Snake's Lost Drum

蛇丟了一面鼓

According to legend, the snake in the old days had a very beautiful drum. He would play very delightful "rrbet, ribet" music.

One day when the snake was playing his drum, a frog overheard it. With jealous thoughts dancing through his head, the frog planned to steal the snake's drum.

Therefore, the frog went to visit the snake to plead, "Dear brother, I heard that you have a beautiful drum that plays very lovely music. My family is having a party in two days. May I borrow it?"

據說，古時候的蛇，有一面非常漂亮的鼓兒，打起來嘓咚嘓咚的響，非常好聽。

有一天，蛇打鼓，被青蛙聽見，起了壞心眼兒，想騙蛇的鼓兒。

於是，青蛙就跳到蛇的家裡，對蛇說：「老哥哥，聽說你有一面漂亮的鼓兒，打起來非常的好聽，過兩天，我家要開慶祝會，能不能借給我用一用？」

蛇説：「好啊！不過，你用完一定要還喔！」青蛙點了點頭，把鼓借走了。

過了好久好久，青蛙一直沒有把鼓兒還給蛇。蛇左等右等，等得很著急，就到青蛙家去要鼓兒。

可是，青蛙捨不得把漂亮的鼓還給蛇，就騙蛇説：「老哥哥啊！我實在太對不起你了。你的鼓打起來眞是太好聽了，我使勁的打，誰知道一個不小心，就把鼓兒打破了。」

The snake said, "Sure! But you have to return it when you're done!" The frog nodded, taking the drum.

After a long, long time, the frog still hadn't returned the drum to the snake. The snake waited and waited. He became very worried. So he went to the frog's house to get the drum back.

But the frog didn't want to return the beautiful drum, so he deceived the snake, "Dear Brother! I am so sorry! Your drum sounded excellent. I played my best, but what do you know, it broke."

蛇聽説心愛的鼓破了，既心疼又生氣。可是，鼓兒既然破了，又有什麼辦法呢？只好悶悶不樂的回家去了。

過了些日子，一天，蛇正躺在床上睡午覺，忽然聽到田野裏傳來嘓咚嘓咚好聽的鼓聲，很像是他的鼓。

When the snake heard that his precious drum had been destroyed, he felt both sad and angry. Yet, since the drum was ruined, what else could he do? So he went home upset.

A few days later, when the snake was lying on his bed taking a nap, he heard "rrbet, ribet" coming from the fields. It sounded like his drum.

The snake slithered out to take a look. It was the frog singing and dancing while playing the snake's beautiful drum.

The snake then realized that he had been tricked by the frog. He angrily confronted the frog, "Hey! Why did you trick me? Give me back my drum!"

蛇走出去一看，原來青蛙正打著自己那面美麗的鼓兒，高興得又唱又跳。

蛇這才知道，自己上了青蛙的當了，走上前，氣鼓鼓的對青蛙說：「喂！你為什麼要騙我，把我的鼓兒還我！」

"Aw! I don't see any drum!" The frog swallowed the drum quickly trying to put off the snake again.

The snake became very angry. So he swallowed the frog along with the drum.

Today, frogs "rrbet, ribet" because the frog stole the snake's drum. Moreover since the frog didn't return the drum, snakes still try to swallow every frog they see.

青蛙連忙把鼓吞下肚去，還想騙蛇。「沒有啊！哪有什麼鼓！」

蛇很生氣，就連蛙帶鼓一口吞了下去。

今天，青蛙所以會嘓咚嘓咚的叫，就是因爲他騙了蛇的那面鼓兒；也因爲青蛙沒有還鼓，所以蛇見了青蛙就開口吞食。

The snake is the sixth animal in the 12-Beast cycle.

Given that most snakes like to eat frogs and frogs make drum-like sounds from their throats, the authors were able to come up with such an imaginative story to explain animal behavior.

Usually people don't like snakes. Actually, if one gets to know more about snakes, they could even become pets. In fact the snake in the story played a generous trusting character, while the small frog played the role of a conniving cheat.

Parental Guide

Ox & Buffalo Change Clothes

黄牛水牛挨衣服

Children sometimes may wonder -- Why don't animals wear any clothes? Don't they ever get cold? Actually, the skin on their bodies are just as warm as clothes. Also, it was said that long ago the skin on their bodies were just like clothes -- They could be put on or taken off. Here is a story about an ox and a water buffalo wearing the wrong clothes.

Legend has it that long, long ago, while the water buffalo wore yellow clothes, the ox wore black clothes. The colors were exactly opposite of the present day oxen and buffalos.

　　小朋友有時候會覺得奇怪——
動物們不穿衣服，會不會覺得冷呢
？其實，牠們身上的皮膚就像衣服
一樣保暖，而且，傳說從前牠們身
上的皮膚，就像衣服一樣，可以穿
穿脫脫呢！這裏，就有一個黃牛和
水牛穿錯衣服的故事。

　　傳說很久很久以前，水牛身上
穿的衣服是黃色的，而黃牛身上穿
的衣服，是黑色的。跟現在看到的
黃牛和水牛的顏色，恰好相反。

How did they put on the wrong clothes? It was like this...

In the past, the water buffalo and the ox were good friends. Since the ox was smaller in size, the buffalo treated him as a little brother. They lived together very comfortably on a large green pasture. Everyday they could eat as much of the crisp green grass as they wanted. The only worry they had came from the tiger raids. Thank goodness God granted them four quick legs. When the tiger showed up, all they had to do was swiftly run away.

牠們為什麼會穿錯衣服呢？原來是這樣的……

從前水牛和黃牛是好朋友，黃牛的個子比較小，水牛便把黃牛當弟弟看待，他們每天都相親相愛的一起過日子。水牛和黃牛住在一片大草原上，每天都可以盡情的吃著脆綠的青草，唯一擔心的是，有時會有老虎來攻擊他們。好在老天爺賜給他們矯健的四條腿，老虎來了，只要撒開腿趕快逃就行了！

One day, it was very warm. After the buffalo and the ox had eaten, they decided to go for a swim. They walked to the pond, took off their clothes and jumped into the water.

"How cool!!!" The buffalo and the ox felt refreshed. While they swam, they chatted. It was so relaxing!

這天，天氣好熱，水牛和黃牛吃飽了，就約好一起去泡水，牠們走到池塘邊，脫下衣服，一下就衝進水裏去。

「好涼快啊！」水牛和黃牛快樂地叫著。牠們一邊泡水，一邊聊天，真是舒服極了！

17

All of a sudden, a "roar" startled them.
"Good grief, no!" the ox screamed. A tiger appeared from behind the bushes next to the pond. The buffalo and the ox hastily made it to shore. They each grabbed their clothes and ran away.

突然間，「吼」的一聲，把他們嚇了一跳。

「媽呀！」黃牛叫了起來。原來，池塘邊的草叢裏竄出一隻老虎。水牛和黃牛急得連忙爬上岸抓起衣服就逃。

After the water buffalo ran for a long, long while, he peeked around to look. Thank goodness, the tiger wasn't following him. When he began to slow down his steps, he realized he wasn't wearing any clothes. Was he ever embarrassed!

When he was about to put on his clothes, he noticed that he had taken the ox's clothes. Now that he had been separated from the ox, what could he do? He couldn't walk around without any clothes! So, the buffalo puzzled over his problem. Reluctantly, he put on the ox's black clothes, but they were much too small. The clothes wrapped tight; it was so uncomfortable. Therefore, he hurried to search for the ox to exchange clothes.

　　水牛跑了好久好久，悄悄回頭一看，還好，老虎還沒追上來，他便慢慢停下腳步。這時他才發現自己沒穿衣服，很不好意思。

　　正要把衣服穿上，又發現拿錯了黃牛的衣服，而黃牛卻跟他跑散了，怎麼辦呢？總不能不穿衣服呀！水牛想想，只好先把黃牛的黑衣穿起來，可是，一穿之下，才發覺太小了，繃在身上好難過呀！於是，就急著去找黃牛換衣服。

What about the ox? Since he was smaller, when he put on the buffalo's yellow clothes, although baggy, they were pretty comfortable. He then came up with a plan to trick the buffalo. He decided to never take off the clothes anymore. But he was afraid that the buffalo would come looking for him, so he hid.

而黃牛呢，他的身材小，穿上水牛的黃衣服，雖然鬆垮垮的，卻覺得滿舒服的。他一時起了壞念頭，便不打算脫下來了。但他又怕水牛來找他換衣服，於是就躲了起來。

水牛要找黃牛，老找不著，心裏很著急。成天嘀咕著：「我要換衣服，我要換衣服。」

這天，水牛終於找到了黃牛，便急著對他叫道：「換呀！換呀！」

黃牛早打定主意不換了，便叫道：「不啦！不啦！」然後飛也似的跑了！

The buffalo searched everywhere for the ox. Yet, he could never find him. He was so anxious that he kept on muttering all day long, "I have to change clothes. I have to change clothes!"

One day, the buffalo finally found the ox. So he rushed over to yell, "Change! Change!"

The ox had already made up his mind not to switch. So he yelled, "No! No!" And as if he had wings on his feet, he ran swiftly away.

The buffalo couldn't do anything. All he could do was to wear the black clothes. But he kept on thinking of his yellow clothes. So all his life he moaned, "Change! Change! (sounds like 'hwan' in Chinese)"

And because the ox wore the buffalo's yellow clothes, he was afraid that one day the buffalo might come for them. Therefore, he nervously cried all his life, "No! No! ('bu' in Chinese)"

Children, next time when you see the water buffalo or the ox, listen carefully to them. Then think of this story. You'll find that it is believable.

水牛沒辦法，只好一直穿著黑衣服過日子，但是他心裏還是很想念他的黃衣服，所以，一輩子都喃喃叫著：「換呀！換呀！」

而黃牛呢，他穿了水牛的黃衣服，就怕水牛找來，因此，一輩子都緊張地叫著：「不啦！不啦！」

小朋友，下次你見到水牛或黃牛，仔細聽聽，是不是這樣叫呢！再想想這個故事，一定會覺得滿有趣的。

This story is not only comical, but also helps the children to learn how the water buffalos and oxen differ from each other.

The excessive skin hanging from the ox contrasts with the sleek taut figure of the buffalo. Because of our advanced technology and transportation, children have limited opportunities to see buffalos and oxen working in fields or transporting cargo. A trip to the zoo or farm can provide children a chance to become more familiar with these animals that have provided mankind with labor and food.

The ox holds second place in the 12 Beasts cycle.

27

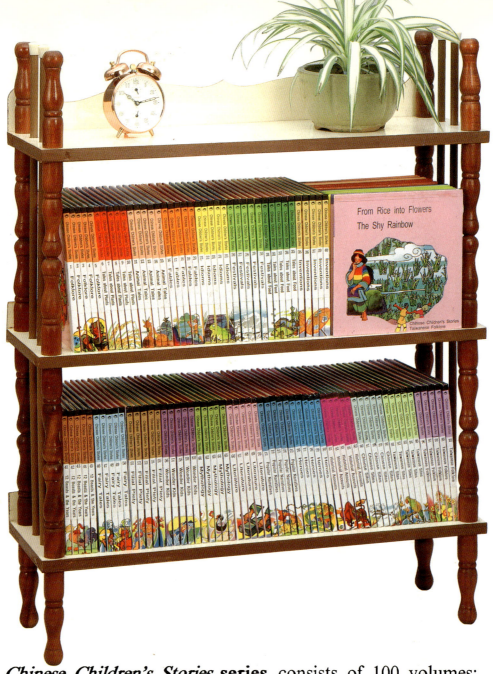

On the spines (left shelf, top): Folklore · Folklore · Folklore · Tales about Plants · Tales about Plants · Animal Tales · Animal Tales · Fables · Fables · Idioms · Idioms · Festivals · Festivals · Tales about Food · Tales about Food · Inventions · Inventions

From Rice into Flowers
The Shy Rainbow

Chinese Children's Stories
Taiwanese Folklore

On the spines (bottom shelf): Beasts & the Years · Fairy Tales · Filial Piety · Wonder Kids · Mythology · Literature · Popular Narratives · Heroes · Historical Accounts · Chinese Sites · Taiwanese Folklore

Chinese Children's Stories **series** consists of 100 volumes;
20 titles of subjects grouped in 5-book sets.

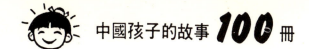

中國孩子的故事 **100** 冊

First edition for the United States
published in 1991 by Wonder Kids Publications
Copyright © Emily Ching and Ko-Shee Ching 1991
Edited by Emily Ching, Ko-Shee Ching, and Dr. Theresa Austin
Chinese version first published 1988 by
Hwa-I Publishing Co.
Taipei, Taiwan, R.O.C.
All rights reserved.
All inquiries should be addressed to:
Wonder Kids Publications
P.O. Box 3485
Cerritos, CA 90703
International Standard Book No. 1-56162-044-0
Library of Congress Catalog Card No. 90-60800
Printed in Taiwan